# Snowball Fight!

by **Jimmy Fallon**

illustrated by **Adam Stower**

DUTTON CHILDREN'S BOOKS

DUTTON CHILDREN'S BOOKS
A division of Penguin Young Readers Group
Published by the Penguin Group
Penguin Group (USA) Inc., 375 Hudson Street, New York, New York 10014, U.S.A
Penguin Group (Canada), 10 Alcorn Avenue, Toronto, Ontario, Canada M4V 3B2
(a division of Pearson Penguin Canada Inc.)
Penguin Books Ltd, 80 Strand, London WC2R 0RL, England
Penguin Ireland, 25 St Stephen's Green, Dublin 2, Ireland (a division of Penguin Books Ltd)
Penguin Group (Australia), 250 Camberwell Road, Camberwell, Victoria 3124, Australia
(a division of Pearson Australia Group Pty Ltd)
Penguin Books India Pvt Ltd, 11 Community Centre, Panchsheel Park, New Delhi-110 017, India
Penguin Group (NZ), Cnr Airborne and Rosedale Roads, Albany, Auckland 1310, New Zealand
(a division of Pearson New Zealand Ltd)
Penguin Books (South Africa) (Pty) Ltd, 24 Sturdee Avenue, Rosebank, Johannesburg 2196, South Africa
Penguin Books Ltd, Registered Offices: 80 Strand, London WC2R 0RL, England

Text copyright © 2005 by St. James Place Inc.
Illustrations copyright © 2005 by Byron Preiss Visual Publications Inc. and St. James Place Inc.

Library of Congress Cataloging-in-Publication Data
Fallon, Jimmy.
Snowball fight/by Jimmy Fallon; illustrated by Adam Stower.—1st ed.
p. cm.
Summary: On a snow day off from school, a young boy cannot wait to have a snowball fight.
ISBN 0-525-47456-0
[1. Snowball—Fiction. 2. Snow—Fiction. 3. Stories in rhyme. 4. Humorous stories.]
I. Stower, Adam, ill. II. Title.
PZ8.3.F213Sn 2005
[E]—dc22 2004025067

Published in the United States by Dutton Children's Books,
a division of Penguin Young Readers Group
345 Hudson Street, New York, New York 10014
www.penguin.com/youngreaders

Designed by Edie Weinberg

Manufactured in China · First Edition
3 5 7 9 10 8 6 4 2

To my elementary school in Saugerties, NY—St. Mary
of the Snow—for giving me and my sister plenty
of snow days to play together

J.F.


For Nan, with love

A.S.

# Snow day! School's closed!

**Snow is white. Half my height!**

# Somewhere, out there, snowball fight!

Snowball,
snowball,
snowball fight!

Long johns.

Moon boots.

**Woolly hats**

**and hand-me-down snowsuit.**

**No time for breakfast,
already late.**

# Pretend I don't hear when Mom yells,

##  "Wait!"

Fort is ready.

**Munitions stored.**

Way too quiet.
Getting bored.

**Spied around but didn't see...**

fifteen snowballs coming at me.

ATTACK!

# Snowball, snowball, snowball fight!

Snowball,
snowball,
snowball fight!

Out of ammo,
trapped in fort.
Enemy approaching,
need support.

Sneak attack. Plan revealed.

**Use your toboggan as a shield.**

# Snowball, snowball, snowball fight!

# Snowball, Snowball, Snowball fight!

**Run back home,
in retreat.**

# Snow down my back, soaking-wet feet.

# Pj's, cocoa, fireside truce.

# One last snowball, future use.